THIS WALKER BOOK BELONGS TO:

_____

_____

_____

_____

For Daniel Goldin

First published 1997 by Walker Books Ltd
87 Vauxhall Walk, London SE11 5HJ

This edition published 2000

10 9 8 7 6 5 4 3

This book has been typeset in
Stempel Schneidler Medium.

Printed in Hong Kong

British Library Cataloguing in Publication Data
A catalogue record for this book is available
from the British Library.

ISBN 0-7445-8114-1 (hb)
ISBN 0-7445-6964-8 (pb)

WILLY THE DREAMER

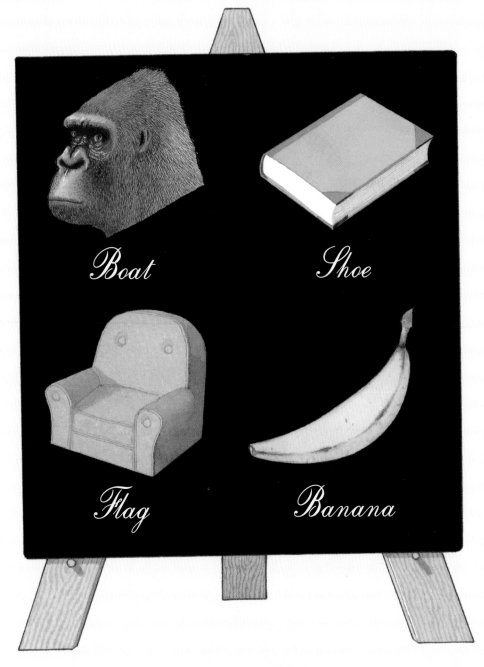

Boat

Shoe

Flag

Banana

Anthony Browne

WALKER BOOKS
AND SUBSIDIARIES
LONDON · BOSTON · SYDNEY

Willy dreams.

Sometimes Willy dreams that he's a film-star,

or a singer,

a sumo wrestler,

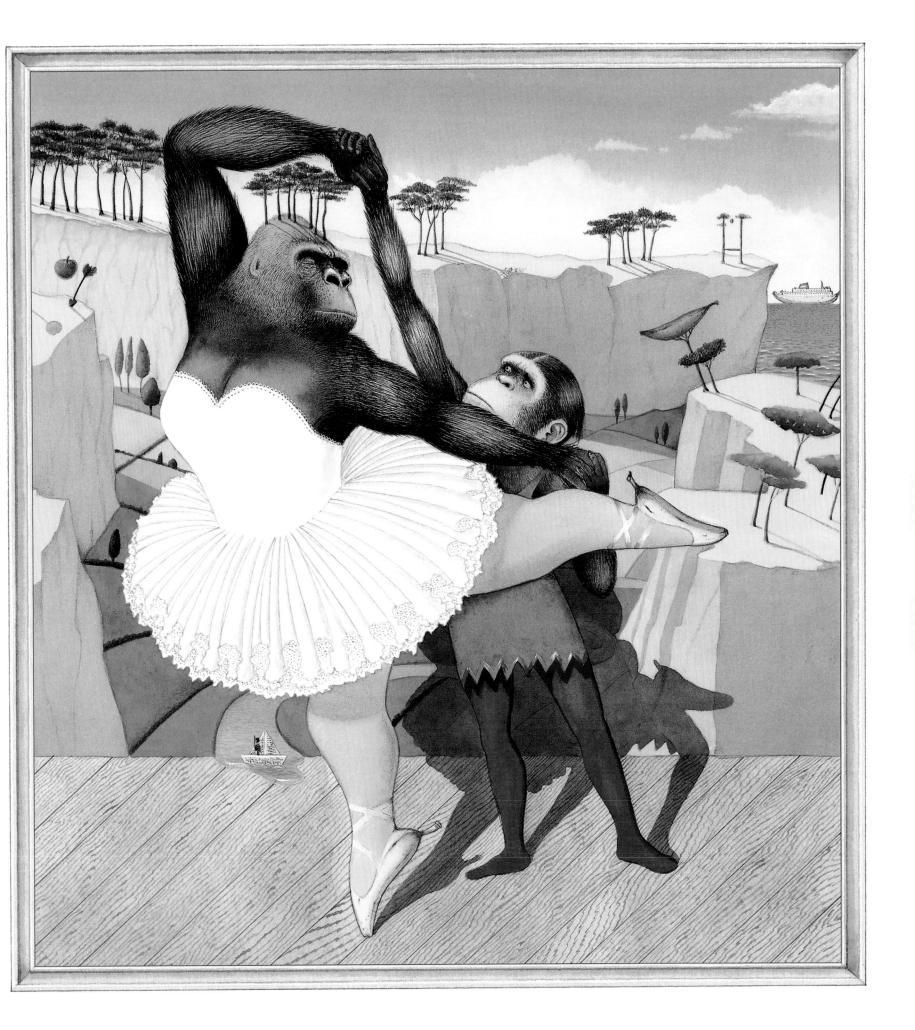

or a ballet dancer... Willy dreams.

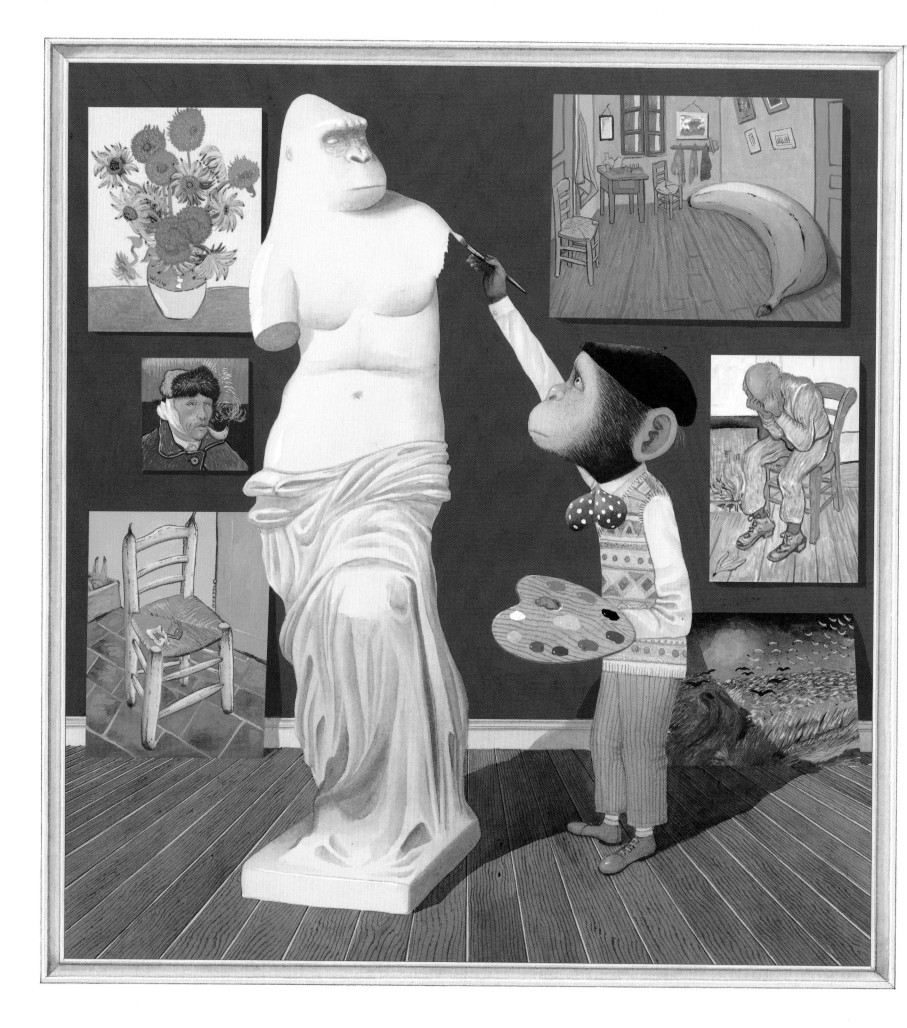

Sometimes Willy dreams that he's a painter,

or an explorer,

a famous writer,

or a scuba-diver... Willy dreams.

Sometimes Willy dreams that he can't run

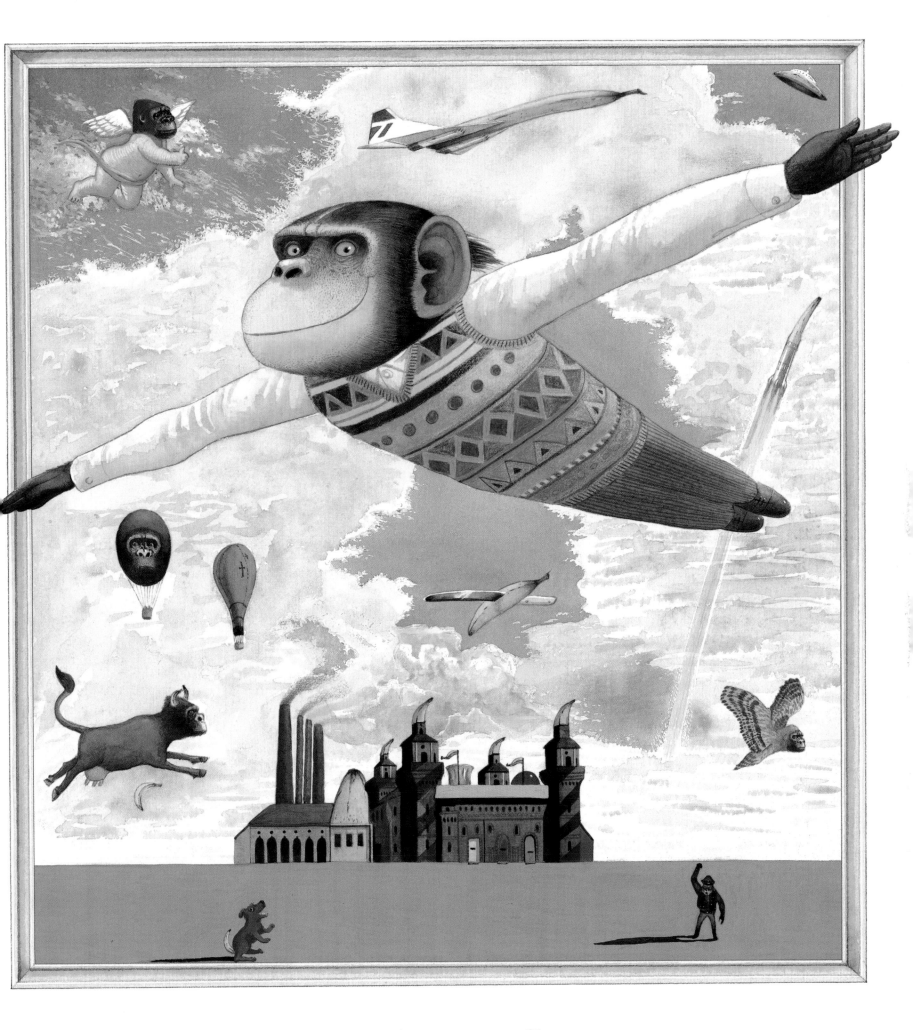

but he can fly.

He's a giant,

or he's tiny... Willy dreams.

Sometimes Willy dreams that he's a beggar,

or a king.

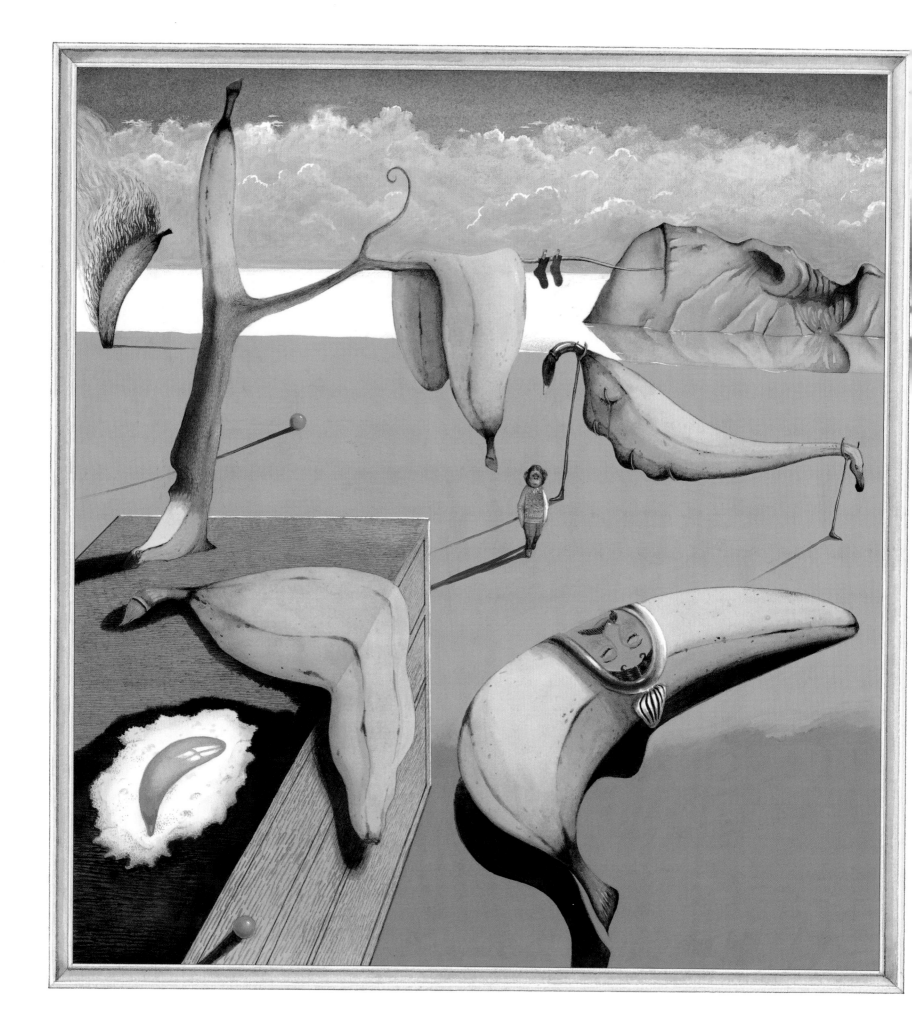

He's in a strange landscape,

or all at sea... Willy dreams.

Sometimes Willy dreams of fierce monsters,

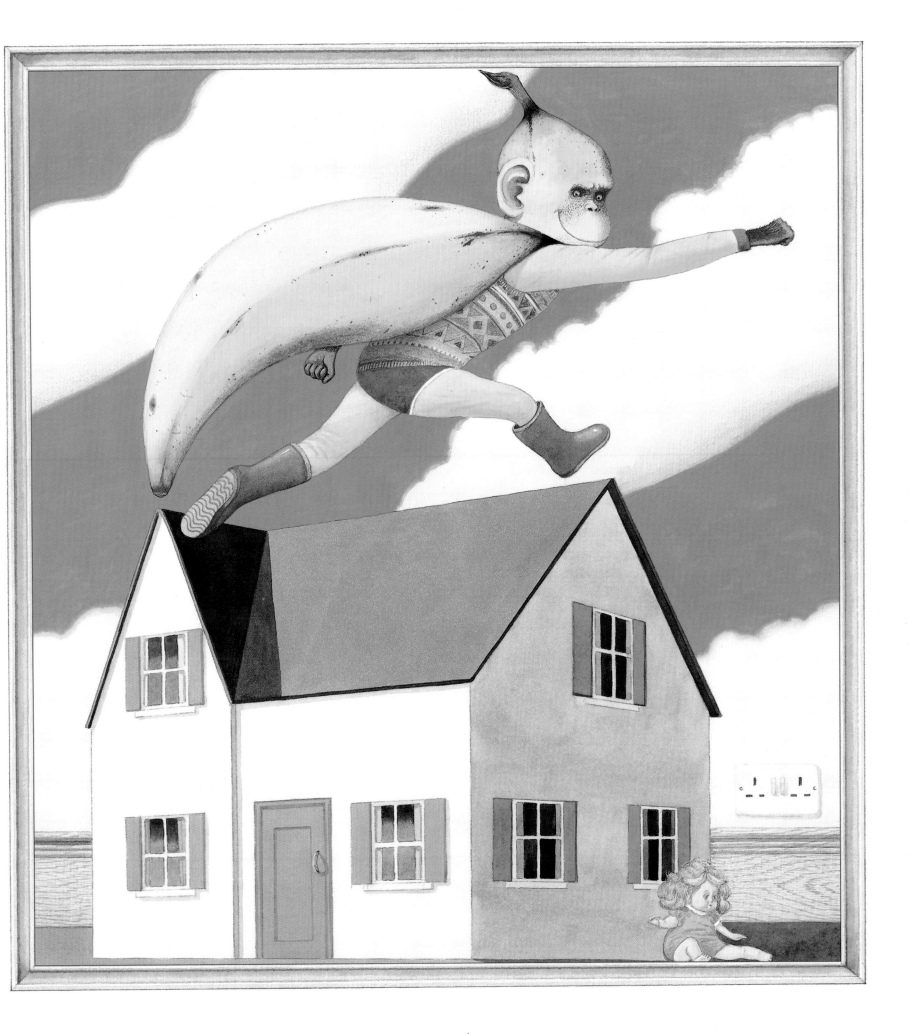

or super-heroes.

He dreams of the past ...

and, sometimes, the future.

Willy dreams.

Willy the Dreamer

ANTHONY BROWNE says of *Willy the Dreamer*, "I had been wanting to do a book about dreams for a long time but I couldn't work out how to do it. Dreams seemed to be an important part of my childhood and the Surrealists' visions of dreams had a powerful effect on me when I was a teenager. I had also been wanting to make a book without a plot – a series of one-off paintings which held together without a story. So I combined these two ideas – dreams and a series of paintings – but how could that be a children's book? The answer was to paint Willy's dreams. It was the most enjoyable book I've ever worked on."

Anthony Browne is one of today's most popular and acclaimed children's artists. In March 2000 he received the highest international distinction for a picture book artist, becoming the first ever British illustrator to win the Hans Christian Andersen Award for Illustration. His many other awards include the Kate Greenaway Medal for *Gorilla* and *Zoo*, and the Kurt Maschler Award for *Gorilla*, *Alice's Adventures in Wonderland* and *Voices in the Park*. *Willy the Dreamer* was shortlisted for the Kate Greenaway Medal. Among his many other books are *Willy the Champ*, *Willy the Wimp*, *The Visitors Who Came to Stay* and *Through the Magic Mirror*. Anthony Browne lives in Kent.

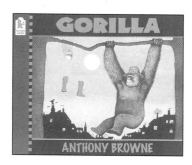

ISBN 0-7445-9997-0 (pb)

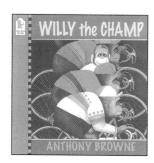

ISBN 0-7445-4356-8 (pb)

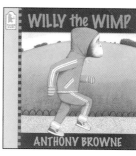

ISBN 0-7445-4363-0 (pb)

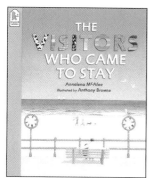

ISBN 0-7445-7706-3 (pb)

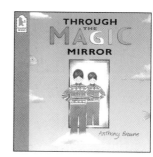

ISBN 0-7445-7707-1 (pb)